THE BEAR WITH NO HAIR

BY JUSTIN READ

ISBN: 9781702254977

HAVE YOU EVER SEEN
A SIGHT SO RARE,
AS A BIG GRIZZLY BEAR
WITHOUT ANY HAIR.

THE ANNOYING THING
FOR A BEAR WITH NO HAIR,
IS THAT A BEAR'S NOT A BEAR
IF A BEAR CANNOT SCARE.

AS HARD AS BEAR TRIED
WITH A ROAR AND RAISED CLAW,
THE OTHER BEARS LAUGHED
AS THEY ROLLED ON THE FLOOR.

BEAR FROZE IN THE WINTER,
BEAR BURNED IN THE SUN,
BEAR FOUND IT HARD
TO SIT ON HIS BARE BUM.

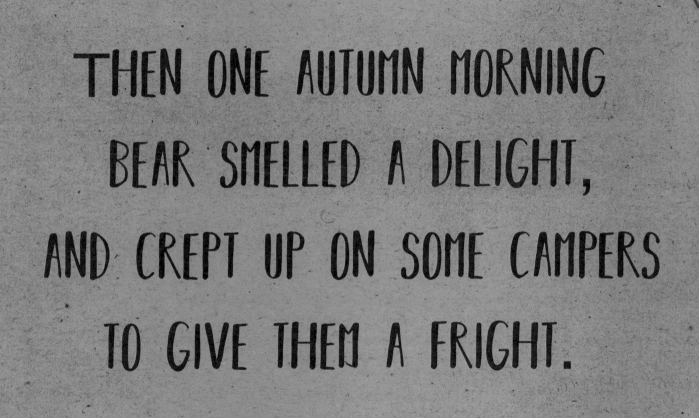

THEN ONE AUTUMN MORNING
BEAR SMELLED A DELIGHT,
AND CREPT UP ON SOME CAMPERS
TO GIVE THEM A FRIGHT.

THE CAMPERS JUST LAUGHED,
AND COULD NOT HELP BUT STARE,
AND THOUGHT TO THEMSELVES,
WHAT WOULD A BARE BEAR
WEAR?

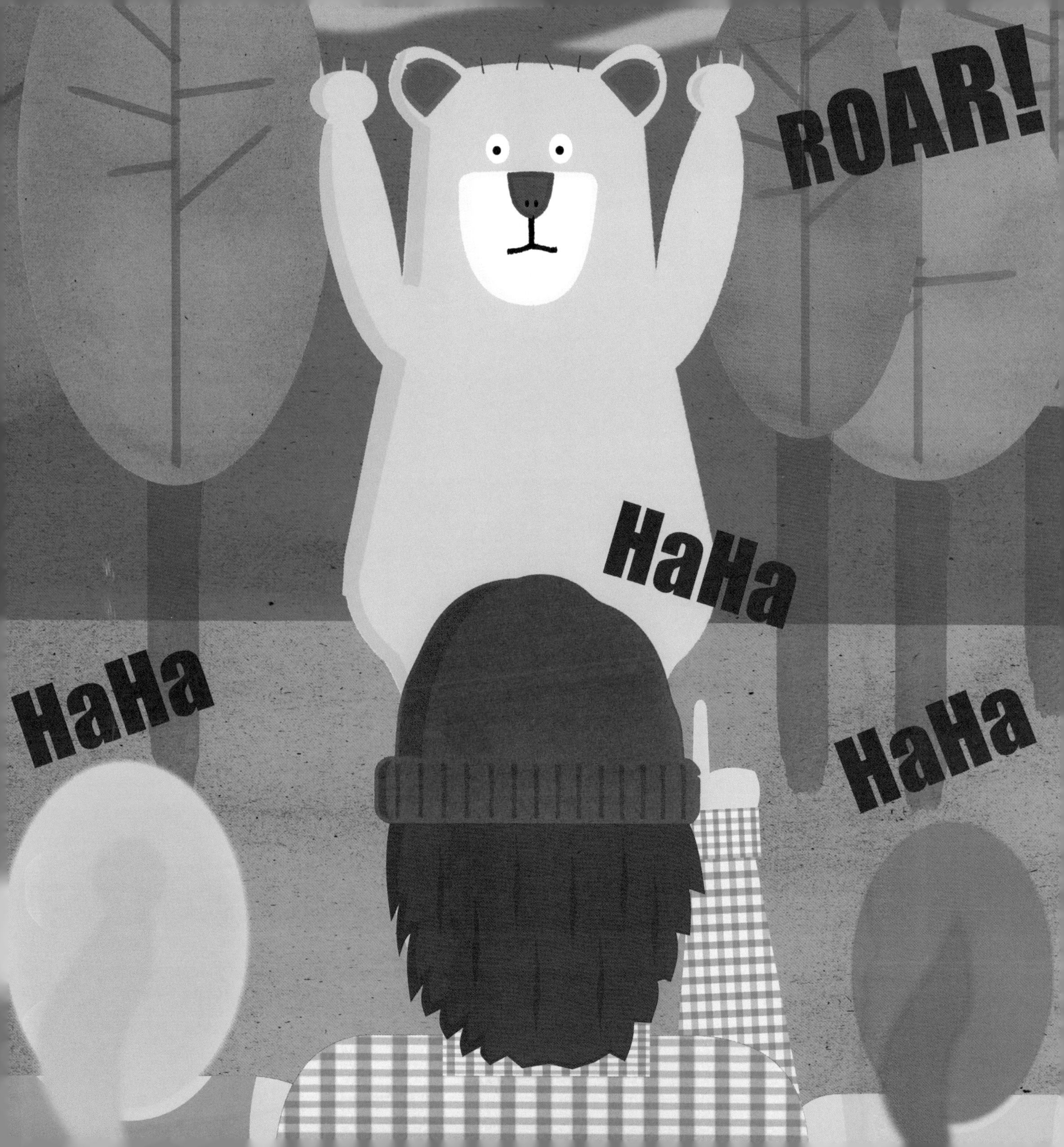
ROAR!
HaHa
HaHa
HaHa

THEY RUMMAGED AROUND
AND PULLED OUT SOME CLOTHES,
THEN COVERED THE BEAR
FROM HIS HEAD TO HIS TOES.

WITH PANTS ON HIS HEAD,
AND THE JEANS A BIT TIGHT,
THIS BIG GRIZZLY BEAR
WAS A REAL FUNNY SIGHT.

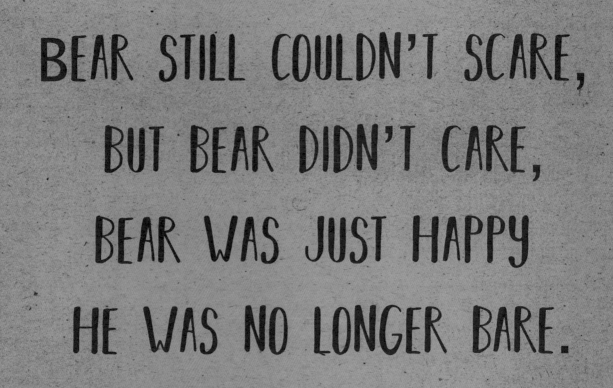

BEAR STILL COULDN'T SCARE,
BUT BEAR DIDN'T CARE,
BEAR WAS JUST HAPPY
HE WAS NO LONGER BARE.

SO WHEN THE COLD FREEZE
OF WINTER
MADE ITS WAY BACK ROUND,
BEAR SLEPT IN HIS CAVE
ALL WARM, SAFE AND SOUND.

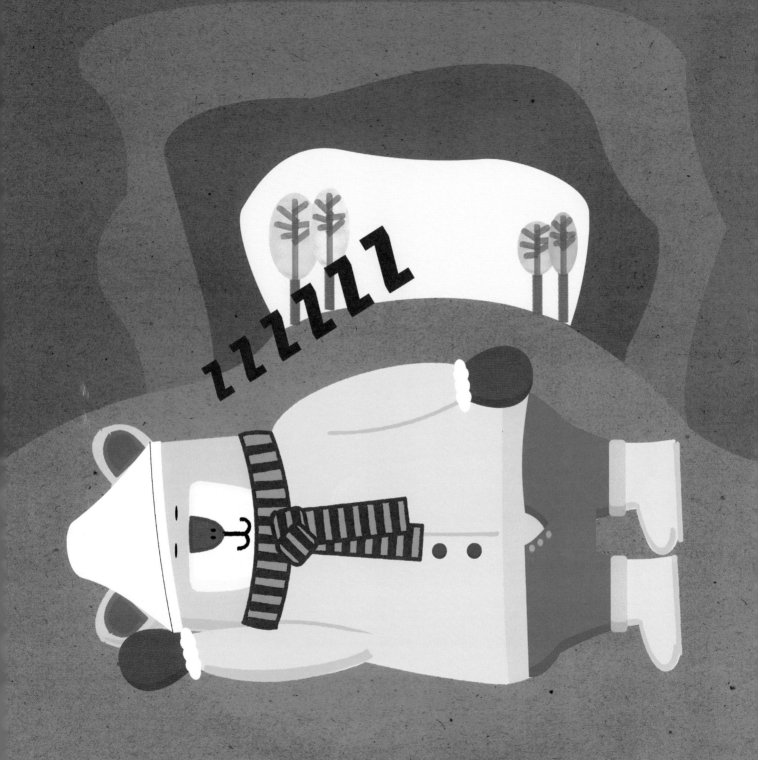

THE END.

ALSO AVAILABLE

Printed in Great Britain
by Amazon